LEGO CITY

FOLLOW THAT EASTER EGG!

By Trey King

Illustrated by Sean Wang

Scholastic Children's Books
Euston House,
24 Eversholt Street,
London NW1 1DB, UK

A division of Scholastic Ltd
London ~ New York ~ Toronto ~ Sydney ~ Auckland
Mexico City ~ New Delhi ~ Hong Kong

This book was first published in the US in 2014 by Scholastic Inc.
Published in the UK by Scholastic Ltd, 2016

ISBN 978 1407 16352 9

LEGO and the LEGO logo are trademarks of the LEGO Group © 2016. All rights reserved.
Produced by Scholastic Inc. under license from the LEGO Group.

Printed and bound in Italy

2 4 6 8 10 9 7 5 3 1

Papers used by Scholastic Children's Books are made from woods grown in sustainable forests.

www.scholastic.co.uk

It is a quiet morning in LEGO® City . . . until the sound of a security alarm rings out! Barry is breaking his friend Larry out of jail!

The crooks lift a manhole cover. They are about to escape into the sewers. "Yuck, that smells!" says Larry. "I think I'd rather go back to prison!"
"Come on!" yells Barry.

Later, Larry and Barry arrive at their hideout. "I remember this place being nicer," says Larry.
"It's no fancy hotel, but it's a great place to hide from the cops," Barry explains.

"I want a nap," says Larry with a yawn.
"We don't have time for naps," snaps Barry. He unrolls a large piece of paper with his plan drawn in crayon.

"Today is Easter, and this plan to steal a golden egg is going to make *me* rich!"
"Don't you mean, make *us* rich?" asks Larry.
"Oh, yeah. . . I meant *us*," says Barry.

Across town, the police chief gives two new cops their first job. "Ryan and Katie, today you'll be driving the armoured car from the bank to the museum."
"We're ready for the challenge, sir," says Katie.

"You better bring Reno, the police dog," says the police chief. "You're guarding a priceless treasure."
"Yes, sir!" says Ryan.

Ryan and Katie don't get far before they have to stop. A traffic light is lying in the middle of the street.

"Why would someone put a traffic light in the middle of the road on purpose?" asks Ryan.

"I don't know, but Reno thinks this smells fishy," says Katie.

While the police are distracted, Larry and Barry break into the armoured car. "What a beauty!" says Barry. "With this golden egg, *I'm* going to be rich!"

"Don't you mean, *we* are going to be rich?" asks Larry.

"Oh, yeah. . . *We* are going to be rich," says Barry.

Reno sees Larry and Barry and barks! Ryan and Katie turn to see the crooks making their getaway. "After them!" shouts Katie.

"Let's hide in that crowd!" says Barry. The two crooks run into the city park. A huge Easter festival is taking place. Everyone is celebrating with games, snacks and lots of painted eggs!

EASTER FESTIVAL

Barry trips and the golden egg flies into the air.
It bounces from one balloon to another.
"Follow that egg!" Barry shouts to Larry.

15

The golden egg lands in a bucket of popcorn. "Yay! I haven't eaten since prison," says Larry. "We're not here for a snack, we're here for the golden egg," Barry says.

As soon as Barry gets the popcorn, a bird flies down and grabs the egg.

"That bird is a thief!" Barry shouts as the bird flies away.

"So are you," Larry says. "Maybe you're related."

The mummy bird flies to her nest high in a tree.
"Maybe she thinks the golden egg is one of hers,"
says Larry. "How cute!"

"It's not cute!" shouts Barry. "She's stealing what we
stole first!"

Barry climbs the tree. But the popcorn butter makes the egg slippery. The egg falls through his fingers!

"*My* egg!" shouts Barry.

"Don't you mean, *our* egg?" asks Larry.

Larry tries to catch the golden egg, but it is too slippery. It bounces from his hands to a sign, and then off a man's head. It finally lands in a giant pile of golden, chocolate eggs.

EASTER FESTIVAL

"A whole pile of golden eggs!" says Barry. "We are going to be rich!"

"Those aren't *real* golden eggs," says a little girl. "Those are chocolate eggs wrapped in gold foil."

"How are we going to figure out which one is the real egg?" asks Larry.

"Let's eat them!" Barry says.

"What a delicious search!" shouts Larry.

"You better slow down or you'll get a tummy ache," says the little girl.

"*Ouch!*" Barry shouts. One of his teeth breaks when he tries to bite the real golden egg.

"You found it!" says Larry.

"And *we* found *you*!" says Officer Katie.

"Does your jail have a dentist?" asks Barry.
"It sure does." Ryan laughs.
"We captured the crooks, saved the golden egg and got free chocolate," says Katie. "What *sweet* success!"